Fingerlings
friendship @ your fingertips

Unicorn Magic

Written by Tori Kosara

Senior Editor Tori Kosara
Proofreader Kayla Dugger
Designers Stefan Georgiou and Thelma-Jane Robb
Jacket Designer Guy Harvey
Pre-production Producer Siu Yin Chan
Producer Lloyd Robertson
Design Manager Guy Harvey
Managing Editor Sarah Harland
Publisher Julie Ferris
Art Director Lisa Lanzarini
Publishing Director Simon Beecroft

Reading Consultant Linda B. Gambrell, Ph.D.

First American Edition, 2019
Published in the United States by DK Publishing
345 Hudson Street, New York, New York 10014

Page design copyright © 2019 Dorling Kindersley Limited
DK, a Division of Penguin Random House LLC
19 20 21 22 23   10 9 8 7 6 5 4 3 2 1
001—314127—Feb/2019

A catalog record for this book is available from the Library of Congress.

ISBN (Paperback): 978-1-4654-8436-9
ISBN (Hardcover): 978-1-4654-8437-6

DK books are available at special discounts when purchased in bulk for sales promotions,
premiums, fund-raising, or educational use. For details, contact: DK Publishing Special Markets,
345 Hudson Street, New York, New York 10014
SpecialSales@dk.com

Printed and bound in China

www.dk.com
www.fingerlings.com

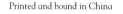

A WORLD OF IDEAS:
SEE ALL THERE IS TO KNOW

Contents

Meet the unicorns

The unicorns are Gigi, Alika, Gemma, Molly, Skye, and Stella. They have magical powers!

Alika

Gigi

Skye

Stella

Gemma

Molly

Sparkle Heights

The unicorns live in a town.
It is named Sparkle Heights.
Everything is made of candy.
Yum!

Sweet home

There are so many sweet things to eat in Sparkle Heights.

Lollipops

Tarts

Gumdrops

Cotton candy clouds

Sprinkles

Cake

Gigi

Gigi loves her friends.
She shares her magic
with them.
Gigi is a good friend.

Skye

Skye uses magic to fly.
She flies above the cotton
candy clouds.
Zoom!

Stella

Stella looks at magic stars.
She makes wishes on them.
Her dreams come true!

Alika

Alika likes sparkles.
She leaves magic sparkles
wherever she goes.

Rainbow magic

Gemma and Molly look
for magic rainbows.
The colors are so pretty!

Gemma

Molly

Best friends

The unicorns are friends.
Friendship is the best magic!

Quiz

1. Where do the unicorns live?

2. What is everything in Sparkle Heights made of?

3. Which unicorn flies over clouds?

4. Who looks for rainbows?

5. What is the best magic of all?

Index

Answers to the quiz on page 22:
1. Sparkle Heights 2. Candy 3. Skye
4. Gemma and Molly 5. Friendship

A LEVEL FOR EVERY READER

This book is part of an exciting four-level reading series to support children in developing the habit of reading widely for both pleasure and information. Each book is designed to develop a child's reading skills, fluency, grammar awareness, and comprehension in order to build confidence and enjoyment when reading.

Ready for a Level 1 (Learning to Read) book
A child should:
- Be familiar with most letters and sounds.
- Understand how to blend sounds together to make words.
- Have an awareness of syllables and rhyming sounds.

A valuable and shared reading experience
For many children, learning to read requires much effort, but adult participation can make reading both fun and easier. Here are a few tips on how to use this book with an early reader:

Check out the contents together:
- Tell the child the book title and talk about what the book might be about.
- Read about the book on the back cover and talk about the contents page to help heighten interest and expectation.
- Chat about the pictures on each page.
- Discuss new or difficult words.

Support the reader:
- Give the book to the young reader to turn the pages.
- If the book seems too hard, support the child by sharing the reading task.

Talk at the end of each page:
- Ask questions about the text and the meaning of the words used—this helps develop comprehension skills.
- Read the quiz at the end of the book and encourage the reader to answer the questions, if necessary, by turning back to the relevant pages to find the answers.

Series consultant, Dr. Linda Gambrell, Distinguished Professor of Education at Clemson University, has served as President of the National Reading Conference, the College Reading Association, and the International Reading Association.